Swingers Party - A Wife Watching Multiple Partner Hotwife Romance Novel

Karly Violet

Published by Karly Violet, 2021.

This is a work of fiction. Similarities to real people, places, or events are entirely coincidental.

SWINGERS PARTY - A WIFE WATCHING MULTIPLE PARTNER HOTWIFE ROMANCE NOVEL

First edition. October 25, 2021.

ISBN: 979-8201300425

Written by Karly Violet.

Swingers Party

A Wife Watching Multiple Partner Hotwife Romance Novel

Chapter One: Old Times

I'm not always one for parties, but when my old college buddies decide to come into town with their families, I can't turn down a mini-reunion with them. "How are the hotdogs coming along?" I ask Brenton as I walk up to where he's standing next to a grill. He's agreed to hold this little get-together at his home since he has the largest yard and the nicest grill.

"They're getting there," he says with a wide smile. His reddish beard glistens in the sunlight as he tends to the hotdogs. I wonder why he ever decided to grow that thing out for summer?

"The kids are starving," Devin, another friend of ours, says as he walks up with a bottle of beer in one hand. "My kids are going apeshit for Uncle Brenton's world famous hotdogs."

"World famous, eh?" Brenton smiles at the complement. "I think your two little ones would probably eat just about anything, Devin. Sort of like you." We all three laugh as Devin shakes his head. Though not out of shape, he has put on a few pounds over the last couple of years. It's good to see him, though. Living more than three hundred miles away in Texas caused me to wonder if he would be able to make it at all.

"Well, they love your hotdogs. So, pronto, Uncle Brenton. Get them ready for the little rascals." Devin smiles as he turns to point at our other friends who have shown up for the backyard party. "You would think that Luther and Aiden have no dicks the way they fawn over their wives. Honestly, not one of them has come over to say hello to us yet."

"They'll get here," I tell my old friend. "Give them a chance to get things settled with their families first. The wives, after all, are the true bosses of our homes."

"Here-here," Brenton agrees as he lifts a bottle of beer toward me. I do the same and he takes a quick drink of it.

"Not my wife. She does what I want her to do." Devin seems very defiant as he looks into my eyes.

"Really? Let's just see how much you have her in your spell, buddy. Hey, Katie? Can you come over here."

"Don't do that."

"Katie." I wave at Devin's beautiful young wife. "Yeah, come here."

"Dammit, Jordan. Do you really have to make a point whenever I say something?"

"But, this is an *important* something," I say with a chuckle as Brenton smiles along with me. I watch as Katie makes her way to the grill.

"Hello boys," she says with a smile on her face. The young woman puts her arm around Devin and kisses him on the cheek.

"I was hoping you could help us figure something out," I say as I try to hold back the laughter that is about to erupt from within me.

"Um, okay. Shoot." Katie is always a good sport whenever I do something to embarrass her husband. Hopefully she will play along now as well.

"Devin seems to be under the impression that he's the boss in your home." I smile wickedly at the two of them.

"I didn't say it like that," Devin says in his defense. He looks at Katie and tells her, "He's just trying to get something started. Ignore him."

"The *boss?*" his wife parrots. "What do you mean?"

"I mean, the *boss.* The one who decides everything in the household. He tells you when to do something, how to do something, and where to do something. You know; the boss."

She nods her head, a smirk gently rising along her lips. "Wow. A boss?" Katie turns to look at Devin. "Are you my boss?"

"Look, baby, it's not as easy as that."

"Sure it is," she presses him. Katie is going right along with my little scheme to get at my old friend. Though Brenton behaves as if he's only interested in how the hotdogs are cooking, I can see that his attention is also on this particular interaction.

"You know how guys talk," Devin begins as he attempts to navigate his way through the mess I have happily created for him. "You know I don't mean what I say."

"That you're the boss? You don't mean that?" Katie raises an eyebrow, her blue eyes focused firmly on her husband.

"Yeah. I don't mean it. I love you, honey." He puts an arm around her.

She sighs. "Well, I don't know. You might have a honey-do list waiting for you at home later. I have to be certain that you don't think yourself too high and mighty for that sort of work, Dev." Katie loves putting the knife in and twisting. I enjoy watching it happen, too. "Be good, sweetie." She gives him a kiss on the cheek before turning and walking back to join her friends.

"Fuck," Devin says as he looks over at me. "You are going to get me killed one of these days when you do that."

I laugh. "Nah. I'll just make sure Katie keeps you in line." Brenton and I have a laugh at his expense as Aiden and Luther finally walk up to us.

"I hear there's a cookout going on here," Aiden says with a smile.

"Hey, man, good to see you." Brenton reaches over and shakes Aiden's hand. We all do the same as we greet Luther as well.

"Thanks for the invite. I was a little surprised, though," Luther adds to the conversation. "I'm all the way in Washington state. Did you really think that I would come?"

"Why not?" I ask as I pat him on the shoulder. "A party wouldn't be a party without you, buddy. We would be without our legendary panty-raiding cowboy."

"Ah, shit," Luther says while shaking his head. "Don't ever tell my wife about that."

"The panty raid?" I say a little louder.

"Be careful with this guy," Devin tells our friend. "He's already gotten me into a honey-do list with Katie. I think he's feeling his own oats with Mindy being gone today."

"Mindy's not here?" Aiden seems disappointed. "You guys live around here, right?"

I nod my head. "Yeah, but she already had a planned business trip this weekend. There really wasn't any way that she could break that off and come along with me."

"Or else I would be figuring out a way to shit on your marriage too," Devin says with a wry grin. "You're a real fucker, you know that?"

I laugh. "We're *all* real fuckers."

"Ah, yes, the panty-raiding and April." Benton smiles widely as he strokes the short hairs of his red beard. "Sweet April."

"Wow, dude, that's going back a little," Luther chuckles. "I almost forgot about her."

"How the hell do you forget about someone like that? Her ta-ta's..." Devin doesn't finish his sentence as he sees Katie nearby watching him. He turns away from her and she offers me a quick wink. She's going to have fun with her husband today.

"Nice rack," Aiden agrees. "Damn, I can't believe we did that, fellas. All of us."

"And probably a few others," I add. "She seemed like the type that wouldn't do that either. When she came in and offered herself the way that she did, it blew my mind." My cock gets a little hard as I remember the spunky, petite blonde who was at the party during the spring semester of our senior year in college. April showed up with some guy named Craig but soon broke it off with him. She chugged beer, did whiskey shots, and I think even went as far as to smoke a little weed in one of the rooms at the fraternity house. Then, one by one, she dared us to fuck her. She wanted to see how many guys could bed her in one night. We were all happy to oblige, though most of us ended up with sloppy seconds and thirds. Normally this sort of thing would have been off-putting to me, but she was just too sexy and I was too drunk to turn her down.

"If Katie knew about her," Devin begins as he looks around to see if his wife is nearby. "She would probably cut my dick off and shove it down my throat."

"You didn't know her then," Brenton chuckles. "It was a college thing. Lots of guys and girls did things in their university days that they wouldn't want others to know about. My wife, for example, has told me that she has some skeletons in her closet, too."

"Sarah? She has skeletons?" Aiden shakes his head. "Impossible. Isn't she like a devout Catholic?"

"We both are," Brenton answers. "So, yeah, we don't screw around now like we did back then. It doesn't mean that it didn't happen, though."

"Sure," I reply in agreement. "It's all in the past. Even the ladies have things they did in college that they don't want to get out to other people."

"You say that, but have you told Mindy about April?" Devin asks. "Does she know that you doggy-styled that girl in college?"

"Oh, yeah. Forgot about that one," Luther laughs. "Damn, you were a real porn star, Jordan. She even moaned while you did that to her."

"Fuck." I shake my head as I think back to what happened between us. April was horny and wanted to try something different, so she got on all fours and I fucked her hard. Really hard. We both came and made a huge mess on that couch in front of a couple of dozen college students.

"I wouldn't mind having a party like that again," Aiden comments. "Maybe even a party with lots of other women."

"Or wives." Devin stops himself. "Don't tell Katie, please."

Our wives?" I laugh. "Damn, you're a daring man, aren't you. Katie would absolutely finish you for thinking something like that."

"A swinger's party?" Luther smiles while shaking his head. "That would be fun. I've known a couple of people who have done that, but I don't think they did it more than once or twice. It's supposedly a great way to give your sex life an extra boost."

"Yeah, a boost toward divorce court," Brenton replies. "I don't think Sarah would go for that sort of crazy idea. She's pretty straight-laced when it comes to sex."

"Straight-laced?" I raise an eyebrow. "How so?"

"Dude." He lifts his grill tongues and wags them in my direction. "Just nevermind that, alright?" The tall, fair-haired man smiles as he pulls the hotdogs off the grill and puts them on a platter nearby. "Anyway, college is behind us. Group sex stuff is behind us. We're all grown with kids now."

"Not me," I answer with a laugh. "No children for the wife and I. Mindy doesn't want any."

"Yeah, well give it a little time." Brenton looks out over the crowd in his backyard and says loudly, "Hotdogs for the kiddos. Come and get it!" Several children come running over to pick up paper plates, buns, and the cooked tubes of meat that Brenton has prepared for them. I watch with fascination as each little pseudo-gremlin gets his or her food and then trots away to eat it. No, I don't need or want kids. Pussy, on the other hand, I'm always ready to have.

"We should have a swingers party," Aiden says with a wicked grin on his face. "My wife might actually go for that."

"Not mine," Brenton says for the second time. "Leave me out of this crazy scheme. Devin, if I were you, I'd be careful of this as well."

"Yeah, careful," he replies while eyeing his wife nearby. "It would be fun, though."

"And crazy. There's no way the ladies would be up for that. We're all just turning thirty years old now and most of us are dragging kids along wherever we go. Times have changed." Luther nods his understanding toward Brenton. "I'm not sure Lydia would do anything like that either."

"It's just a pipe dream anyway," I say with a chuckle. "Just talk amongst buddies on a hot summer day in Brenton's back yard." I reach into a cooler to pull out another bottle of beer. "Let's just try to enjoy it." I raise my bottle after opening it and most of the guys do the same before we all take a drink. The thought of young, sexy April's ass in my hands from eight years ago continues to make me hard as I sip the cold ale. I wish I could go back and fuck her for a second time, but that will never happen. I'm sure she's moved on and gotten married since our college days as well. Besides, she likely has worked hard to forget about what happened that night at the party. Most would have.

Chapter Two: Great in Bed

"You know, I missed you while you were gone," I say to Mindy as she gets into bed beside me.

We kiss for a moment before she asks, "Did you behave yourself while I was gone, Jordan?" My wife is five-two, weighs about a hundred pounds, and has short blonde hair with green eyes. To say she's a sexual dynamo is an understatement. As she moves her hands into my shorts, I begin to wonder if she's going to show me just how much she missed me in a moment.

"I was good," I tell her as she wraps her small fingers around my hardening pole. "Fuck, honey. You're a little tease."

Mindy smiles. "I had to masturbate twice while I was gone because of how horny I was, sweetie. Do you know what it's like to lie back on a hotel bed and play with yourself?" She sees the look on my face and quickly adds, "Never mind."

I laugh. "Did you have a naughty dream about me a time or two, baby?"

"Maybe." My wife pulls up hard on my pecker, causing me to pre-come as my body shudders in the bed. "Did you have any dreams about me?"

"Fuck, yes," I growl as I reach out and pull her breasts out of the small bra she is wearing. I play with her small pink nipples as she fondles my pocket rocket. When Mindy wants to play, she plays.

"Do I make you horny?" Mindy giggles as she releases my cock and stands up at the side of the bed. She finishes pulling off her bra and the small panties she is wearing. Her beautiful trimmed beaver glistens as she waits for me to take off my own sleep shorts. After I do, she goes down on me and begins to suck on my dick.

"Oh, I missed that," I tell her as the tip of my shaft reaches the back of her throat. "Damn, Mindy, you are so fucking talented." Looping my fingers through her short blonde hair, I imagine April going down on me the same way. She did, just before I fucked her from behind all those years ago. Since reminiscing with the guys about our time at that party,

I have had a hard time forgetting the young woman we all took turns in bed with.

My wife lifts her head and looks at me. "So, you and your college buddies had a nice barbecue at Brenton's house, right?" She turns back and kisses my cock.

"Um, yeah. It was fun. I wish you had been there." My balls ache as Mindy toys with my little man.

She then asks, "What did you guys talk about?" My wife turns and goes back down on me, my cock throbbing as she wedges it snuggly inside her throat before lifting her head and going back down again. At this rate, she'll have me spewing like a volcano.

"We, uh, talked about the old days." I close my eyes as I try to get April out of my mind. Dammit, she's going to cause me to say something to Mindy that I don't want to say.

"And?" My wife takes a brief break before going back down again. This time, her hand massages my balls.

"Shit." My body shakes as Mindy gently moves along my pole. She knows that I can't refuse whatever she wants while she's giving me a blow job. "We talked about parties we used to go to," I say to her. My wife moves around and straddles my face, lowering her pussy to me so that I can lap at her sweet nectar. The aroma of her musky vagina causes me to harden even more as I kiss her clit and then lick at the moisture surrounding it.

"Jordan," she moans as she lifts her mouth from me and gently grinds her pussy into my face. Mindy loves to have sixty-nine with me and it seems that tonight she's in the mood for a good tongue lashing.

"We talked about a girl too," I manage to tell her as she goes back down on me and lifts her ass just slightly. I quickly go back to licking and sucking at her ladybit as Mindy lowers her muff back to my face. This is how we continue for the next few minutes, our bodies enjoying what is happening between the two of us. I love Mindy with all my heart, but sex often takes precedent in my mind whenever I'm as horny as I am now. April continues to fill my thoughts as my wife sucks on my cock.

Mindy lifts her mouth from me and looks back. "A girl? What about a girl? Tell me, Jordan. I want to know." She smiles wickedly at me before going back down on my erect phallus. My wife keeps her ass up just out of reach of my mouth as she licks the length of my pole.

"Fuck, you're going to make me tell you," I grunt as I move around beneath her. Though I know better, I want to share the story with Mindy. It turns me on to let her know that I've fucked other women in much the same way it turns me on to know that she's fucked other men. "Her name was April," I say breathlessly. "There was a party our senior year of college and she was there." I gulp hard as I catch the scent of her beautiful pussy again. "Honey…" I reach up and use my hands to pull her down to me. I again begin to lick and nip at her sweet beaver.

"Jordan," Mindy moans after she lifts her face from my crotch. "Tell me more. I want to know what happened at the party. I want to know about April." She moves her pussy around in my face before pulling it up again. My wife then goes down and sucks even harder on me, causing my toes to point hard.

"April," I say as I feel goosebumps rise all over my body. "She really liked sex." Licking my lips, I continue, "Some of the guys had sex with her during the party. They sort of passed her around."

Mindy stops and lifts her mouth from my shaft. "Passed her around?"

I wince as she rubs my dick with her hand. "Well, she went from one guy to the next for sex." More goosebumps arise along my body. Why am I telling her this? Mindy isn't the sort to be free of jealousy. There's been a time or two that she's caught me looking at other women and then used that to batter me verbally for weeks at a time.

"Did *you* have sex with her?" Mindy asks me directly.

I take a quick breath. "Honey, you have to understand…"

"Did you fuck her, Jordan?" My wife's tone is sharp. She has figured me out and she won't take a silly non-answer this time. No, I have to tell her what happened.

"Yes," I say quietly. For a moment, Mindy stops rubbing my dick and I begin to wonder if we're about to have a huge fight. However, she soon starts rubbing me again.

"And, did you like it? Be honest, Jordan. It's alright." Her pussy drips a little as I watch it from a few inches away. Is she really getting into the idea of this?

"Um, yes," I tell her. My wife then lowers her pussy and allows me to begin licking her again before she goes back down on me. We are back to having sixty-nine sex together, which surprises me a little. I just admitted to having sex with another woman. What's going on?

"Oh..." Mindy lifts her mouth as her body begins to undulate with an orgasm. "Don't stop, Jordan...oh..." I pull her clit into my mouth and begin suck gently onto it. *"OHHHH!!!"* Her labia become a little darker and get wetter as I keep sucking on her. *"Jordan...uhhhh...ohhh, baby...ohhhh..."* Mindy grinds her pussy into my face as she comes. Her mouth quickly engulfs my manhood as she continues to orgasm and it doesn't take long for me to begin to fill her mouth with my salty gravy.

"MMMMMMMMM!!!" Her pussy covers my nose and mouth as I come with her. *"Mmmmm...MMMMMM!!!"* I struggle to catch a breath as I keep spurting into my wifes throat, but she soon lifts herself so that I can finish enjoying what's happening without passing out. *"Fuck...oh, fuck..."* Mindy finishes me off and swallows every drop of my spunk before getting off of me and dropping to the bed beside me. We both breathe hard as we take in the afterglow of the moment.

"You *fucked* her?" Mindy looks over at me as she breathes hard.

"Well, yeah. It was before I knew you," I reply. "I'm sorry."

"Don't be." My wife reaches over and plays with my wilting pecker as she asks, "What position did you like most with her?"

I laugh nervously. Are these questions her way of getting me on some marital technicality that she can take to an attorney and use against me? Though I doubt as much, I am worried about where this is going. Still, I answer her, "Doggy style. That's how I came with her."

"Did she come too?" Mindy focuses hard on me as she rolls closer and puts her hand on my chest. "You can tell me, Jordan. I'm just curious, that's all."

After swallowing hard, I reply, "Yeah, I think so. At least, it felt and sounded like she did." My cock begins to get a little hard again as I admit all of this to my wife. It makes me horny to share this sort of stuff with her, and I get the feeling that it makes her horny as well.

"Good. I'm glad that you liked it." My wife kisses my cheek as she pulls on my cock. She then pulls back a little and tells me, "Just don't do it again, alright? You played in college and so did I. We're beyond that now." Mindy smiles before getting out of bed and going to the bathroom. As she closes the door, I think about the conversation I had with the guys in Brenton's back yard.

"Not happening," I say as my body shakes from the anxiety the admission has caused me. "They want a swinger's party and my wife would probably rather swallow razors than ever take part in something like that. It was just a stupid thing to talk about anyway." If I were perfectly honest with myself and my wife, I would tell her about the swingers party idea. However, I can't be honest to any point further than what I have already been. Though the thought of me having sex with another woman before I ever met her probably makes her a little horny, Mindy would never willingly allow me to do that again. I can't blame her. I'm not sure how I would react if I saw her with another man. So, as far as the swinging thing goes, it's not going to happen.

Resting back on my pillow, I consider how lucky I've been over the years whenever it comes to sex. I've always had a very physical partner, which I consider myself fortunate to have. However, I made the decision to settle down with Mindy when we got married and that's just the way it has to be. Even if I do occasionally think about April and how she let me screw her from behind eight years ago.

Chapter Three: Not Kidding Around

I've always held an interest in software and software development. Even as a kid, I would tinker on a computer and try to figure out the coding to some basic programs that I had downloaded. My father would constantly gripe at me about the dangers of computer viruses or other things getting onto the family desktop computer. They never did. Probably because I was always a little ahead of my parents when it came to keeping the computer secure.

"Great program, Jordan." Peter Davidson, the project manager on our new line of heart rate monitors, smiles at me as he stops by my cubicle. "It's streamlined and very user friendly. Our clients will be happy with what they purchase." He has a seat next to my desk. "So, what would you like to work on next? We have a couple of new projects opening up soon. One of them, as you know, involves a new wearable medical bracelet that electronically shares information to medics and doctors. The other is the new MRI machine we're putting together. Either one is yours, according to Dr. Weston." Dr. Jennifer Weston is our company chief executive officer. A former surgeon, she decided in her forties that she wanted to be on the other end of medical equipment innovation.

"I don't know. Maybe a break?" We both laugh a little as Peter nods his head.

"You've earned one, huh? What you did to restructure the basic skeletal framework of the programming language will advance other products here as well. With less bulk for the software, we can advertise the huge advantages of storing patient data in the device. Hospitals and clinics will clamor for the updated monitors."

"That's good to know." The company has treated me well since I joined more than five years ago. I have become their lead software developer and engineer, surpassing even some of the more seasoned people at the company. Though that has upset a few people in my department, most understand why I've risen in the company the way that I have. Peter knows all too well how people can talk, though. He also made his way up the corporate ladder here in a hurry.

"Take a couple of days and think about which one you prefer, Jordan. Just shoot me an email or come by my office to let me know." The young executive stands to his feet.

"I will." As I nod at him, Peter turns and walks away.

My phone almost immediately rings and I pull it from my shirt pocket. "Hello?"

"Hey, Jordan." The voice is too familiar. It's my friend, Aiden. "I thought I would give you a quick call this morning. Are you busy right now or can you talk?"

I look over the sides of my cubicle. I don't have any close neighbors in the large room, and there are some taking their morning breaks already. "Sure. What's up?"

Aiden clears his voice on the other end. "I've been thinking a little and talking to Rebecca."

"Your wife?"

"Yeah, you remember her, right?" It's hard to forget a woman like Rebecca, also known as Becky to her friends. She's tall, athletic, and tan. How the hell Aiden ended up with her is one of those mysteries in life I will probably never understand.

"I remember her from the last backyard barbecue," I reply.

"Good." I get the sense that my friend is being a little cagey with whatever it is that he wants to say to me. Though he has called me, it's as if I'm the one who called him and has asked him some difficult question.

"Okay, man, what's up?" I say again.

Aiden sighs. "Rebecca and I discussed what we talked about at the party at Brenton's place. She's open to the idea."

"The idea of what?" I say with confusion.

He replies in a hushed tone, "The swingers thing."

My heart races as my eyes widen and my cock stiffens. "Um, *what?*"

Aiden clears his throat. "My wife is willing to consider swinging at a party. She thinks it would be fun and kinky."

"Holy shit," I say quietly. Standing to my feet immediately, I look around to make certain that no one has heard me. "You're joking, right?" I sit back down in my chair.

"I'm not joking," he answers. "Look, Rebecca and I have been trying to find something to do to spice up our marriage for a while now. This swinging thing might just be what we need to jumpstart our marriage. Let's be honest, Jordan. We could all use this."

"I can't believe what you are saying." Though I have fantasized about what it would be like to actually go through with a swingers party in our group, there is no way that I could actually go through with it. Mindy would have my head on a pike if I were to seriously consider such a thing. Just the other night she told me that what happened with April at the party in college doesn't mean much to her. She also said that I am to never do that sort of thing again.

"Believe it. Also, I think Devin's wife might be a willing participant from what he told me last night while we were texting."

"Katie?!" Now my heart is racing to the point that I wonder whether I might pass out. "Are you sure?"

"Very sure," he answers. "Jordan, it's as if the stars are aligning and we might just get to do this! Who would have thought that before the barbecue?"

"It was all just talk," I tell him. "Aiden, we were just bullshitting while we talked about April and the party in college. We can't do this. It would cause too much trouble for us all."

"Have you told your wife about April?" The question doesn't surprise me.

"I told her. I even told her about our swingers talk just yesterday morning. She's okay with the April story, but not with the idea of swinging. Mindy even threatened me should I ever have sex with another woman. That would sort of defeat the purpose of a swingers party, Aiden."

He chuckles. "Well, I guess so. Still, you might be able to convince her, right? Maybe one or two of the wives?"

"Geez, how many are willing again?"

"One or two. Rebecca for certain. Maybe Devin's wife."

"But maybe not her." I'm sensing that Aiden might be reaching for straws here.

"He thinks that she will, like I said. You need to speak to him yourself, though. Maybe you should call Luther as well."

"Hell no. I'm not going to try to get everyone to agree to let other men screw their wives." My voice rises again and I stop to stand and look over the cubicle walls for a second time. Thankfully, I'm still not noticed by those working nearby. Most are probably wearing earbuds and listening to music or podcasts anyway.

"It's got to be you," Aiden replies. "You're the guy we all look too, after all. If you can get Devin and Luther on board, then we can turn our attention to Brenton and Sarah."

I laugh. "You know they won't do that. They're devout Catholics, Aiden. Very devout. I mean, Brenton helps the padre in his church on Saturdays to do work around the church buildings. They aren't going to strip down and screw other people at a party." I keep my voice down this time as I can hear other people coming back in from their breaks. The last thing I need is to have to explain to human resources what I was talking about on the phone at my desk today.

"Just talk to Devin, alright? See if his wife is actually serious about this and then move on to Luther. These two guys are really influential with Brenton, right? Use them to get him and his wife to agree to do it. We need to have this party!" Aiden's horniness is on full display in our phone call as he presses me to try to get a swingers party going for us. It really doesn't matter, though. Even if Devin's and Luther's wives are game for such a thing, Mindy certainly is not. If she were to discover that I was planning a swingers party, she would go ballistic. I'll be damned if I'm going to have my wife going after me because of some half-baked scheme like a swingers party.

"I'm sorry, man. I just don't think that's a very good idea. I have my own wife to consider."

"For fuck's sake, Jordan. You used to have more balls than this." He sighs heavily and adds, "Alright. I'll talk to you later."

"Later." We hang up and I put my cell phone on the desk in front of me. The idea of swinging makes me horny just as Aiden is horny for it. "I want to do it," I say quietly to myself before admitting, "Mindy isn't going to go for it, though. You can't piss her off, Jordan." Pursing my lips together, I think about Rebecca and how sexy she is. It wouldn't bother me in the least to go deep into Aiden's wife while she's bent over a sofa. It also wouldn't upset me if Katie, Devin's wife, wanted to wrap her full lips around my johnson. Though I'm sure Aiden is aggravated with me for refusing to go along with this, he has to understand that I would be happy to plan and host the damned party if only Mindy would agree. That's the kicker, though. She won't.

"Hey," Peter says as he comes by my cubicle. "Dr. Weston really wants you on the wearable device if you're game. You still have a choice, of course, but she wants her best person on the software for the wearable. I think it might be a nice change of scenery for you as well."

I nod my head. "I was thinking that very same thing myself. Sure, I'll do it."

Peter smiles. "Good to hear, Jordan. I'll let her know." He taps the top of my cubicle wall before turning and walking away. At least now I'll have something to focus on instead of what Aiden called about this morning. Considering that I still have a hardon in my pants, that could be a good thing or a bad thing. It turns out that I love software development so much that it sometimes gives me a woody.

I smile. "Down boy." Standing to my feet, I pick up a notepad to cover my bulging pants. It's time to pay a visit to the men's restroom where the orgasm fairies await.

Chapter Four: A Life of Its Own

23

I get home right after work and Mindy is sitting at the dining room table eating a snack. After putting my keys on a shelf near the front door, I make my way to her and have a seat nearby. "How was work?" I ask as I smile at her.

"It was okay," she tells me. "I had to fire someone today." My wife works as a human resources manager at a retail corporation headquarters in the city. Sometimes she tells me about those she lets go on a typical day. I've been thankful on occasion that she's not my HR manager.

"What did they do to get fired?" I ask as I clasp my hands on top of the table.

She shrugs her shoulders. "It was an older employee who has worked for the company for more than twenty years. We found out that he was watching porn on a company computer and that it's likely been going on for a while." Mindy raises her eyebrows as she looks over at me. "You don't do that at work, do you?"

I laugh. "Nah, I look at porn here at home to keep from getting fired." Though I find my comment hilarious, my wife doesn't even crack a smile.

"He's been there for so long," she continues solemnly. "He was a good employee other than that, too. His sales numbers were among the highest in the company. But he was so stupid as to use his company computer to look up filthy websites and gawk at them. Why would a guy do that, Jordan? Why would someone with such a successful career take it and flush it down the toilet for something like that?" Mindy is obviously upset that she had to fire this man today. Sure, it was stupid of him to surf porn at work, but there are lots of guys who at some point in their careers do the exact same thing. Thankfully, most of us don't get caught.

"I'm sorry about all that. He must have been a good guy?"

"Yeah, he was." Mindy grimaces before looking into my eyes and smiling at me. "So, how was your day?"

"It was okay," I reply with a nervous grin. Thoughts of my conversation on the phone today keep running through my mind. "I spoke to Aiden for a few minutes during my morning break."

"On the phone?" I nod my head. "How's he doing?"

"Good," I reply. "Rebecca is just fine as well." Mindy knows Rebecca, but not all that well. She's met her a couple of times and they seemed to get along pretty well together, but they're not what I would call close friends.

"That's nice." My wife takes a drink of water before continuing, "So, what did you guys talk about?" This is the very thing that I've worried about all day. Mindy and I always discuss our friends and many of the conversations that we have, but practically none of them have been so risque in the past. What Aiden said to me today is a little different than most conversations I've had with him. How do I begin to tell my wife what we talked about?

"You know, usual guy stuff," I answer at first. "Aiden had a lot to say about what we talked about at the party over at Brenton's house."

Mindy raises an eyebrow. "When you talked about that girl in college?" I nod my head. "That must have been an interesting discussion." She can see that I'm struggling to let her know exactly what was said. My wife is one of the most gifted people I have ever met when it comes to reading someone. It's probably why she makes such a great human resources manager.

"I guess you could say that," I respond. "But, it went even further." After swallowing hard, I tell her, "Aiden says that he and Rebecca are very open to the idea of having a swinging party with the guys and their wives." My heart races as I watch Mindy's facial expression change.

"Really? Both of them?"

"Yeah. They want to put together a swinger's party, and he claims that Devin and his wife Katie are interested as well." My mouth becomes dry and I clench it shut. Mindy is beginning to understand much better what I am talking about.

"A party with all of you guys and us wives?" Mindy's green eyes settle on me in a sharp glare. "Uh, no. Not happening. You've got to be teasing, right?"

"Teasing?"

She shakes her head. "You know what I'm talking about, Jordan. The swingers thing is a kink of yours, I get it, but not something that anyone would seriously consider doing."

"Lots of people do that," I reply. "Something like ten or fifteen percent of married couples swing at some point in their marriages."

Her green eyes again set upon me and I begin to realize that this conversation isn't as simple as I had hoped that it would be. "You are out of your fucking mind. I'm not having sex with Aiden, Devin, or any of your other buddies. And you're not going to have sex with their wives." Mindy stands up from her chair. "After what I just told you about work today, you have the audacity to ask if I would take part in a swingers party?" She turns and walks toward the kitchen to put her empty glass down on the countertop next to the sink.

"It's just something that we talked about," I say as I get up and follow her. "I didn't say we were going to set a party up, honey. Aiden called and told me his wife is good with doing that, and Devin appears to be ready with his wife. That's it. Nothing has been planned."

"So, you're not thinking about going ahead with this?" Mindy puts her hands on her hips and waits for my response.

"I don't know. I thought I would ask you first since you are pretty open to other things."

"No, dammit. What the fuck is wrong with you?" My wife throws her hands up as she shakes her head. "Why would you think that I might do this, Jordan? When have we ever even talked about it?"

I shrug my shoulders. "There's been a couple of times during sex that we have talked about having someone in bed with us. You get turned on during that kind of talk."

"No, I don't," she answers fiercely. "I don't like the idea of having sex with other people. I've only ever just gone along with you to help you get off." The admission stuns me as I gasp. Do I really need to be lied to in order for me to orgasm? Seriously?

"That's not nice," I tell her. "You know that we've both enjoyed talking about different things during sex, Mindy. We've both had fantasies and we've both shared them. Why does the thought of swinging with other couples bother you so much? You're normally cool about talking over things." I catch myself a little too late as I remember something she once told me. It's obvious why she doesn't like the idea.

My wife lets out a breath and answers, "The fact that you want to have sex with another woman besides me at all concerns me. Jordan, are you really that tired of me?"

I shake my head. "I will never get tired of you." Reaching out, I put a hand on one of my wife's crossed arms. "Sex between us has always been good, right? I love to be with you in bed. It's just an idea that was brought up by the guys and that apparently some of their wives have said they would go along with. I'm not looking to replace you or anything like that." The look in Mindy's eyes causes goosebumps to rise along my neck and shoulders. She seems genuinely hurt by the idea that I might want to screw any other woman at all.

"There won't be any swingers party, Jordan. Promise me that." With her green eyes fixed upon me, there's no way that I can turn down such a promise. I nod my head and she then pulls away from me to go to our bedroom. She closes the door behind her and I turn to make my way toward the living room.

"Fuck me," I say to myself as I sit down on the recliner. "I've pissed her off." My cell phone buzzes inside my pocket and I pull it out. It's Aiden once again, undoubtedly anxious to know if I've spoken to Mindy yet.

"Hey, did you two talk?" He texts me.

Sighing, I type in the text message box, "I told her about what you said and she told me that she would never do that sort of thing. She even got a little angry with me." I send the text and look around to make certain that my wife hasn't come into the living room.

"She has to agree, Jordan. Devin wants it and his wife wants it. Luther will be on board with this soon. We need you both to make this a real party."

"Brenton?" I ask.

A frowning face emoji returns and then text follows. "He wouldn't even talk to me about it. The guy is really serious about being faithful to his wife, even if it's not really a question of faithfulness if she's there with him."

"I told you," I text back to him. "My wife too. I don't think I can talk about this much more. If Mindy finds out that I'm still discussing this, she might get pretty hurt by it."

"Why?" I have never told my buddies what reason I believe has kept my wife from at least considering a swingers party between us. It just never felt like something that needed to be said until now.

"Mindy's parents divorced when she was thirteen because her father ran off with another woman," I reply in a text message.

"Yeah, I know. And?"

My fingers shake as I begin to reply to Aiden's latest text message. If I tell him now, there's no going back. The cat will be out of the bag. Mindy, if she were to find out that I have shared this information, would likely not forgive me anytime soon. I don't want to tell my old friend the entire story, but I feel like I have to. It would make his understanding of our situation more complete.

"Her parents were swingers for a brief time. Her dad met another wife and they skipped out of town. She didn't see him again for two years, and by then he had divorced her mother and married the other woman. So, it's a sore subject to begin with." My heart pounds hard as I share the story with him. "Keep this to yourself," I tell him as an afterthought.

"Fuck," is his reply. "I can see why she doesn't want to be a part of this, man. I'm sorry." I put my phone down on the desktop. A part of me wishes that I hadn't brought up the swinging thing with Mindy. What good has it served? I knew better than to do that to begin with.

"I've got to go," I message my friend back.

"We'll talk later." Aiden and I have finished our conversation and I have a lot to do to make up for the way I have made my wife feel. She honestly seems to think that I want to have sex with someone else simply because she is no longer an adequate fuck for me. Nothing could be further from the truth.

"I'm sorry, baby," I say quietly as I look back at our bedroom. Mindy is most likely taking a shower by now. She prefers to have the daily grime washed off her body before bed so that she sleeps better. I tend to be the same way. Seeing a need to try to reconcile with her, I get up and walk to the bedroom door. As I go in, I hear the shower already running. That's okay. We can talk after she's finished.

Chapter Five: Coming to a Consensus

I've been busy this morning with work, so I don't mind the break that a phone call from Luther gives me as I sit down in my cubicle. "Good morning," I hear his voice say over the phone.

"Good morning," I reply as I smile. "How are things with you?"

"Things are looking up," my old college chum replies. "And for you?"

"Eh, work. You know how that can be."

"Yep. I've just finished up a big project here that was giving me a headache for weeks." Luther is an architect and owns his own firm on the west coast. He is often deep into drawing out some project, even though he has a team of five other architects who work for him. "I'm looking for a little fun soon, my friend. How goes your talks with Mindy?" I quickly realize what he's going on about.

"You spoke to Devin?"

"Aiden," he replies. "You know, they've convinced their wives to go along with this, right?"

I swallow hard as I stand to my feet and look around the room. Though my cubicle offers some privacy, there's always the chance that someone will overhear me on the phone with Luther.

"And Brenton?" I ask. I don't know why I bother since my own wife is completely opposed to anything like a swingers party.

Luther sighs. "Brenton will take more convincing. I think Devin has been talking to him, but he still can't get the man to go along with this. Even the April thing from college is something that he won't talk about much now that we aren't together and he's not buzzed from the beer he was drinking."

"Does his wife even know?"

"Sarah?" Luther chuckles. "I'm sure that she does. Even so, that's a past life for Brenton. He doesn't want to talk about having anything sexual to do with another woman right now. Devin swears that he can get him to agree, though. At least to a soft swap or something like that."

I chuckle. "Well, Mindy's not really into the same thing, so that's not an option for her." My wife has never been that open to anything involving other people sexually. We've had a few conversations during sex that I thought were somewhat productive in that area, but nothing that gives me any hope for getting her to take part in a swingers party.

"You have to keep working on her," Luther tells me. "Swinging isn't as taboo as it once was. People do it a lot now. The statistics say that up to ten percent of married couples have done something like swinging. That's huge, my friend. It's okay to do it now. No one will judge you for it."

"No one but Brenton and his wife." We both laugh. It's strange to think that Brenton was probably the wildest of our group throughout college. If there was drinking and fucking to be done, he was the first to do it. He didn't hold back with April when we all took turns with her in college.

"Talk to Mindy again. She probably wants to do this but feels like it might take something away from your marriage. You need to take her to some of the swinger websites where there are testimonials from people who say that swinging has actually made their marriages better. Trust me on this, Jordan. I did just that and Lydia soon agreed with me. She's actually looking forward to a swingers party now."

I sigh. "After the conversation I had with Mindy a couple of days ago, I'm not sure that she will feel the same way. I'll try, though."

"That's all you can do." After a brief pause, Luther tells me, "Hey, I've got to go now. I'll talk to you later, buddy."

"Yeah. We'll talk later." I hang up with my old friend and just sit back in my cubicle as I stare at my computer screen. What he said makes sense, but I still doubt my ability to convince my wife to go along with having sex with other people. On the contrary, she seems genuinely hurt that I would even want to do something like that. How to approach her again escapes me. Maybe something will change with Mindy's ideas on swinging, but I really doubt it.

My phone buzzes again. I pick it up and lift it to my ear. "Hello?"

"Hey, bro, it's Devin."

"Hey, Dev. Just got off the phone with Luther."

"I talked to him last night." He takes a breath before asking, "Did you get her to agree to do it, or what?"

I chuckle. "I just told Luther that I didn't. Mindy is set in her ways on this, Devin. It's not looking good."

"Well, Katie is really worked up about it," he tells me. "I've not seen her so turned on by anything in my life."

"Katie?" I'm surprised. I've always seen her as being a little like Sarah in most things that have to do with sensuality.

"Yeah. Look, she's already a little bit of a nympho in the bedroom, Jordan. I mean, she's wild when she really wants to be."

I shake my head. "Honestly? Are we talking about the same woman?"

Devin laughs. "Man, my wife has it going on. Katie might look like a prim and proper woman, but when we close the door and dim the lights, she's my little pencil sharpener." We both laugh at the perverse use of imagery on my friend's part.

"Okay. Well, none of that has rubbed off on Mindy yet. She hates the swinging thing because of something that happened in her own family years ago. Her parents did a little of that and it ended with her father going off with one of the women he was screwing."

"Ouch," he replies. "That makes sense, huh? No wonder she doesn't want to do this."

"I've spoken to Mindy and tried to get her to see how it could be good for us and our marriage, but she won't budge. I don't really want to keep pressing her because of her past experiences with her own father, either. I'm not sure what to do."

"You have to talk to her some more," Devin replies. "She needs to know that you are not her father. You're not going to leave her just because you have a little sex with someone else."

"You mean, for example, I wouldn't run off with Katie after having sex with her." My cock hardens as I talk to my friend about screwing his wife. Something about the naughty example excites me deeply.

Devin laughs. "Honestly, Katie wants to ride you hard, Jordan. If you get this set up, you'll have fun with her. I would love to see you with her and I would like to take a turn with Mindy as well." Here we are, two men talking about fucking each other's wives. I want now more than ever to get this swingers party going so that we can actually do this.

"It will take a lot more convincing for Mindy. Probably even more convincing for Brenton and his wife. It won't be all that easy."

"Maybe not, but it would be well worth it, Jordan. Keep it up." I hear someone talking in the background before Devin says, "Hey, the little lady wants to go for a swim with me. You know what that means later, right?" Though I can't see it, I imagine that there's a huge smile on my friend's face. It seems that what I've thought about Katie has been wrong all along. She's not the prude that I imagined. My hardness throbs for her and I hope that soon I will get the chance to see her in action.

"I'll talk to you later, Dev. Have a good one." We hang up and I sit back in my little cubicle. Brenton and Sarah may be the holdouts that my buddies see as the problem, but I see Mindy as my largest stumbling block to getting to have the swingers party go on. She doesn't even want to consider the idea that we could have sex with other people. Her father made that decision for her when he left her mother for a woman he had been swinging with.

"Dammit," I say in frustration as I shake my head.

"Problems?" Laney Fischer, a coworker from a cubicle nearby, looks over the side of my office area.

I shake my head. "Not really. Well, I don't know." Looking at the attractive young woman, I ask, "How do you get a woman to do something that she doesn't want to do at first? I mean, how would I go about convincing my wife that something is a good idea when she's completely against it?" I would normally not converse with someone in the office about Mindy or our relationship, but Laney has always been a great conversationalist. As a matter of fact, I would love it if she were to decide to be more than just a coworker.

She smiles as she leans against my cubicle wall. "That's a tough one. What sort of thing is it that you want her to agree to do?" Her blue eyes stare at me and I feel my skin prickle with goosebumps.

"Um, well, she just doesn't want to do something with some friends that we have. They want to have a party and Mindy is dead set against it. She doesn't like to socialize sometimes."

Laney raises an eyebrow. "I saw your wife at the Christmas party last year. She didn't seem to me like someone who doesn't like socializing with people," she points out. "Are you sure that's the problem?" The young woman is cunning when given something to think about. It's why she's a part of the company's research department.

I sigh. "She just doesn't want to have this party. I'm not sure why," I lie, "But what can I do to get her to at least consider it?"

Laney nods her head. "Women like to be assured that they will be safe when they're going to do something uncomfortable," she begins. "You know, it's easy for a lady to feel like she's been left out for the wolves. Even if her boyfriend or husband is with her, she might get the sense that she really isn't being watched over very well. If there is someone in that group of people that she doesn't want to be around, for example, it might mean that you have to guarantee her that she has nothing to worry about." Laney smiles as her cheeks turn a little red. "You took me under your wing for a few days when I first got here, Jordan. You made sure that everyone was respectful to me and you showed me the ropes here at the company. That went a long way to assuage my concerns about working here. I know that you have it inside you to do it for your wife." My cock flexes inside my pants a little as I hear the young woman speak. She's right. I did an amazing job during her first couple of weeks here to make certain that she fit right in.

"I'll take that advice," I say with a smile. "Maybe I can get Mindy to agree to have the party with our friends after all."

"Am I invited?" Laney asks. I pre-come a little as I think about her question. I want so badly to invite her and to fuck her, but I'm sure that's not what would convince my wife to attend such a party.

"It's just a small get-together with people my wife and I know. I wish you could come, though. If it were up to me, I would be happy to invite you."

"I understand," she replies with a nod of her head. "I'll see you later, Jordan. Try to have a better day." Laney turns and walks back to her cubicle as my mind races through the possibilities of having sex with the young woman. "No, not now," I tell myself. I need to figure out what to say or do with Mindy. She needs assurances that she'll be safe, and that means that I won't leave her for one of the other wives. After all, that's what bothers her about her father's wayward past. If I can convince her of my faithfulness, Mindy will surely agree to the party. It's worth the effort to find out.

Chapter Six: A Good Reason

"The crab cakes are delicious," Mindy says after taking a sip of her wine. We don't often get the opportunity to dine out together, so when my wife told me that she wanted to go out tonight, I immediately called and reserved a table at *Shay's on the Lake*.

"They really are good. I'm not one to normally like this sort of thing, either." I like fish. That's about all I like from the ocean. Lobster, crabs, shrimp, and other things that look too much to me like bugs are just not my thing. Normally. But I wanted to make my wife a little happier tonight, so I'm eating crab cakes.

"Thanks for taking me out," she says with a smile on her face. "It's been a tough week at work and I needed this time out with you." Mindy's face is glowing as she enjoys her meal at the nice restaurant. I feel a little guilty at this moment that I've not taken her out more often.

"You deserve it," I reply. Fidgeting a little, I consider what Laney said to me earlier today at the office. I need to convince my wife that she can trust me if she gives in to the idea of the swingers party. There isn't a woman around who could ever lure me into leaving Mindy and being only with her. No, this isn't at all about a new relationship to me. I want to experience sex with other women while my wife has sex with other men. It would be fun to watch Mindy with Devin or even with Brenton. If only Brenton and his wife would agree.

Mindy looks at me and says, "You're thinking about something. What is it?" Her sweet smile causes me to nod my head and blush a little. She knows me so well.

"Just something," I say at first. "I don't know where to begin or what to say to you."

She leans forward after taking a drink of her wine. "You can talk to me about anything, sweetheart. You know that, right? We're married, for better or for worse. Is it something at work that bothers you?" Mindy takes another bite of crab cake as she looks over at me.

My heart beats hard inside my chest as I sit up straight. Determined to man up to what I need to say, I tell her, "You know that I'll always be faithful to you, right?"

There's a confused look that crosses Mindy's face as she puts her fork down on her plate. "Okay. Yes, I know that." My wife is confused, as would I be if I were on the other end of this conversation.

"And you know that I would never do anything to cause you to see me as any less of the man you married, right?"

"Where's this going?" she asks as her eyes bore into me. I feel compelled to look away for a moment, but then I turn my attention back to her.

Swallowing hard, I ask, "Is there any way that you would reconsider the thing we have been talking about?" Looking around, I can see that there are other diners nearby. It would be terrible if they were to hear me mention swinging or a swingers party. The embarrassment for us both would be awful.

"The thing?" It takes a moment, but then Mindy realizes what I'm talking about. "Geez, Jordan. Why?" My wife shakes her head. I can see that I've upset her with my question.

"It's just that I've been talking with the guys," I say as I try to figure out how to phrase things in the best light. "Devin and Luther both have their wives ready to have the party. Even Aiden and his wife are willing and able to attend."

"That party isn't a party," Mindy says as she looks around as well. She too appears to realize how easy it would be for others to hear anything we say about this matter. "Call it what it is, Jordan. It's a terrible thing to do. After what Dad did to my mother..."

"I'm *not* your father," I say quietly. "I'm your husband. I'm Jordan. I'm the guy who has been faithful to you from the very first moment that I met you. Honey, I would never stray from our vows. You know that."

"But, you want to do *that*. You want to do things with other women." She shakes her head. Mindy wants so badly to just say what she wants to say without worrying about others overhearing us. Perhaps I have chosen the wrong venue for this conversation.

"I think we would both have fun," I reply. "Devin and Katie are really happy about the idea. If she likes the idea of it, you could too."

"Her father didn't do what mine did, Jordan. That's not how I want my marriage to end up." I notice that a man at a table nearby looks at us for a moment before turning his attention back to his meal. He heard us. He knows that we're having a deeply intimate conversation that we should probably have elsewhere.

"I'm sorry about that, my love. I'm not your father, though. You have to get to where you separate the two of us. Even though they didn't work out, it's not our fate. We're a different couple and we have different needs and desires. Please just think about it more without dismissing it outright. Can't you do that for me?"

"Can't you just drop it?" My wife retorts. She puts down her napkin and gets up from her seat. She walks through the restaurant to where the restrooms are located and disappears inside. I'm left to my own thoughts.

"Shit, man," I say under my breath so that the other diners can't hear me. "You're fucking this up. Get things straight. Work it out. You can do this." Mindy is sexually adventurous when she wants to be. We once had sex in a park in the middle of the day. Of course, she was wearing a short skirt and it appeared that she was simply sitting on top of me at first. Anyone walking by, though, would have known that her rising and falling in my lap meant that we were screwing each other. That was in our first year of marriage. Things like that just don't happen with us anymore.

Mindy soon returns from the restroom and has a seat across the table from me. She puts her napkin back into her lap and takes a bite of her food. She appears to be finished with our conversation, her eyes affixed on what she's eating rather than on me.

"Honey," I say after watching her for a moment. "I swear. You have nothing to worry about with me. I'm always faithful to you. I swear it. Please tell me how to make you believe that I could never leave you."

Mindy looks up at me and sits silently for a moment. I try to gauge just what she might be thinking right now, but I can't. My wife is stoic and simply shakes her head as she pushes away her plate and puts her hands on the table in front of her. I'm not sure that I've ever seen her like this before.

"What you're asking me to do is to let you be selfish, Jordan. You want me to give in to what you want and just let you screw one of the other wives. Or maybe all of them. I don't know." I notice that a couple of other diners are now looking at our table. Mindy is speaking loudly enough that there's no doubt about whether they have heard her.

"Please, honey, I…"

"I've told you over and over that I'm not willing to do that. I've tried to be as understanding as I can of the fantasy that you obviously have, but I can't just roll over and give in to this. My father left my mother for another woman that he was swinging with," she tells me again. "Another woman, Jordan. Swinging with other couples is what led my parents to split up and divorce. It wasn't an affair that he quietly had behind her back. It was right in front of her that it was happening. My dad was having sex with that woman while my mother was having sex with her husband. It was a recipe for a disaster that led to a little girl not getting to spend her younger years with both parents in the home. It was a terrible thing to go through and I don't want to repeat that mistake. No, Jordan, I don't want to go to a swingers party."

My face burns with redness as I see several people in the dining room looking at the two of us. I'm now the bad guy and they are more than willing to convict me of my sins just by looking at me. What the fuck can I do? Mindy has decided to excoriate me publicly and there is no way that we will ever be able to come back to this restaurant.

"Okay," I say softly as I look down at my hands. Our server comes by and lays the ticket down on our table. She doesn't have to say anything as she walks away. They want us to pay up and leave as soon as we can. The conversation between Mindy and I is just too R-rated for the management at this establishment.

I pick up the ticket and the little black book it is inside of and look it over before pulling cash from my wallet. I pay for our meals and include gratuity as well before we get up and walk out of the restaurant. My mind swims with what I can possibly say to Mindy now that we are out of earshot of the other diners.

"That was embarrassing," I eventually say to my wife as we get into the car. I purse my lips tightly together as I sit back and shake my head.

Mindy starts the car and puts it into drive. We begin to move down the street, both of us quiet as I continue to just stare out the passengers side door window. What the hell did she do? Why did she *torch* me like that? I tried to be gracious and thoughtful about how I spoke to her, yet she blew up on me. She was angry and maybe even a little condescending. I'm not her fucking father, after all. I consider myself a better man. Maybe she does not.

"Why would you do that?" I finally ask as we drive down Main Street. "Why not just tell me that we would talk about it at home later? You know that I would never do that to you, Mindy."

My wife allows for a quick breath. "You didn't give me a choice, Jordan. You kept on and on about the whole thing. You even brought Katie's name into it."

"Only because it's true," I retort. "I would have never put you out there in front of those other people like that, though. I was trying to keep things just between us, but you decided to let the others in the restaurant think that I'm a disgusting, horny guy."

"Aren't you?" Mindy looks over at me quickly before turning her attention back to the road. "You say that you care about me and that you're faithful, but you won't let this swingers thing go. Even after all you know about my parents and what happened with them, you can't seem to move on. It seems that you are a horny guy after all. Right?" It's a rhetorical question, and one I wouldn't care to answer anyway. The point is, Mindy's upset and she wants to hurt me because of it. Still, why?

"I'll drop it," I say quietly. "You want me to let it go, I will. It's sad, though. When we first got married, you told me that you wanted us to be honest with each other about how we felt about things and what we wanted to do. That included in and out of bed. I've done that and you've taken it as a personal attack on you. Mindy, what you did in that restaurant was harsh. Sure, you didn't like that I brought that up again, but you could have handled it differently."

"We both could have," she says flatly. I decide to not respond as Mindy continues to drive us home. I would have never thought that such a nice outing as a couple could have turned into what it did. It's likely that this idea of a swingers party will not take place with either of us involved.

Chapter Seven: One More Agrees

We don't do it much, but tonight all of us finally get to sit down and enjoy a round of beers and conversation. It's nice to be away from home and the cold stares Mindy has been giving me for the last week. Things have been tough for the both of us, though I've become committed to simply dropping the swinging idea altogether.

"I have something to say," Brenton says as he looks at his bottle of beer on the table in front of him. Devin was the first to get here and to secure a booth in the corner of the bar large enough to seat all of us guys. "I can't believe what it is that I'm going to say," he adds as he licks his lips quickly and shakes his head.

"Go ahead," Luther says with a chuckle. "I already know, but they don't."

"What don't we know?" Aiden asks as he shifts his eyes over to the tall, ginger-bearded man.

Brenton takes a quick breath. "I've been talking to Sarah, and I think we're willing to maybe have that party with you and your wives after all."

"Wait," Devin says as his eyes light up. "Are we talking about the swinging party or something else?"

Brenton chuckles. "You know exactly what I mean."

"Damn." Devin sits back in the booth and shakes his head. "I mean, what the hell happened? You were both so against it, man."

He shrugs his shoulders. "You're right. Neither one of us liked the idea of it at first, but then again we have been talking to Luther and Lydia as well as a few of our other friends..." Brenton's voice trails off momentarily before he continues, "Sarah and I have talked to each other about being more open about things for a while. Sure, we have our own beliefs on marriage, but it's not as if we would be cheating on each other, right? We would be doing things that are agreed upon before we ever do them. It's okay if that's the case, isn't it?"

"Very okay." Aiden chuckles. "Holy shit, I can't believe that you two are really willing to do this with us. That will make things so awesome."

"With the exception of one other," I say as I shake my head. "Mindy won't budge on it. I've tried talking to her and things actually got worse between us. I pissed her off and she let me have it in the middle of *Shay's by the Lake.*"

"Fancy place," Brenton replies.

"Yeah, really fancy." Luther looks across the table at me. "Did she threaten to leave you if you decide to be a part of the party?"

"I can't be a part of it without her, no matter what she thinks. It wouldn't be right. Besides, everyone else is bringing a wife, right? How well would it sit with you guys if I'm having sex with your wife and you can't do the same with mine?" We all laugh. "Well, I can't do that to Mindy anyway. There are just too many bad memories with what happened between her mother and father."

"What happened?" I suddenly realize that Brenton hasn't heard the story.

"Her father left her mother when she was pretty young," I reply. "They had been swinging with another couple and apparently Mindy's dad decided the other wife was a better match for him. Before her mother knew something was going on, her father was already gone with the other woman. She grew up rarely seeing him because of the swinging they were doing with the other couple."

"It wasn't the swinging that caused it," Devin claims. "You know that her father was probably already looking at the other woman before they ran away together. He probably used the swinging as an excuse to get closer to her and then to get out of his own marriage. Most swingers have very strong marriages." My friend has been researching the swinging lifestyle and how people in it feel about their experiences. I have no doubt that he's found this tidbit of information on a swinging website.

"Still, Mindy blames that for ultimately destroying her parents' marriage. It's hard to argue with that logic when it hits so close to home."

"I know what you mean," Brenton replies. "Sarah and I have seen a couple of marriages go bad over the last few years. In one of the couples, both people were cheating on each other at the same time, so we didn't have much sympathy for them. But the other couple had a tough go of it. They loved each other, but they simply wanted different paths for themselves. We felt terrible for them." He sighs before adding, "That second couple convinced us to look into swinging."

"They were swingers?" Aiden says with surprise.

"No, but they told us that basically their sex life fizzled and they just quit being intimate with each other. They told Sarah and I that we should do whatever we could to keep things hot and interesting. The wife in that relationship even said that if they had simply been sexually adventurous, things might have ended differently for them. Sarah and I have been feeling that our sex life has been a little dry for a while."

Luther chuckles. "Well, it seemed like that's what the two of you wanted, man. Just missionary style and once per week, right?"

Brenton smiles. "We thought that was what marriage should be like, but we've decided that we need to do more together. We want to be a part of the party."

"Say it all," Devin goads him. "Come on. You know you want to. Say it, Brenton." I can't help but laugh a little as I watch him squirm in his seat.

"Dammit."

"Come on," Aiden says to Brenton. "You need to say it out loud so that it sticks."

"Shit. Okay, we want to swing. Alright? Satisfied?"

"Very," Luther laughs.

Brenton turns his attention to me. "I think Sarah needs to talk to Mindy. The two of them probably share a lot of the same concerns, Jordan. If Sarah is willing to have sex with one of you guys, maybe she can convince your wife that it's really not such a bad idea. Marriages need a great sex life, and I think that having a swingers party once in a while can do just that. Besides, it's not as if we don't know each other. I know you guys are all clean."

"Except for Luther," Aiden declares with a laugh. "That guy has cooties." We laugh and then we each reach for our bottles of beer. As we drink, I think about what Brenton is offering. If only Sarah could convince Mindy that a swingers party is okay. That could work. However, if it didn't, she might become even more upset with me.

"When?" I ask Brenton.

"When can she see her?" He shrugs his shoulders. "I would guess just as soon as possible. Sarah doesn't have to be back at work for the next couple of days. I'm sure she could drop by your house and see Mindy."

"But, will she be okay with doing that? You're offering to put her out there with Mindy even though my wife might be unwilling to talk about swinging. I'm serious when I say that she's not happy with me, Brenton. I don't want to ruin whatever relationship they have over this."

"Their relationship will be just fine, Jordan. We all know that wives change their minds all the time, and it's normally after another wife has spoken to them."

"He's right," Aiden chimes in. "My girl was dead set against it until Katie called and spoke to her. Now she's worked up about it." He smiles before putting the beer bottle to his lips and taking a sip.

"Sarah can talk to her," Brenton tells me again. "Just give her a chance to get through to Mindy. Women have a way about them when it comes to speaking to their friends. We men just don't have the same magic touch."

"Apparently not," I say while nodding my head. "Okay, let's do it. See if Sarah can come over and talk to Mindy for me. I'd like to see that."

"You want to be there?" I nod my head. "That's fine, then. I'm sure Sarah won't mind." He reaches over and puts a hand on my shoulders. "Leave this to her, Jordan. Things will be different for Mindy by the time Sarah has finished talking to her."

"I'm sure you're right." I have no choice but to put my faith in Sarah when it comes to Mindy and the question of whether we will be a part of the swingers party the group wants to put on. Up until just now, I was convinced that I would have to simply drop the whole thing to get back into my wife's good graces. However, it seems that one semi-prudish woman might be just what I need to get the ball rolling again. Maybe Mindy will listen to her, then again maybe she won't. We can't know for certain until she tries.

"Anyone tried calling April?" Luther looks around at the rest of us.

"April who?" Devin replies before he suddenly realizes who our friend is talking about. "The same girl from that party years ago? *That April?* Do you even know her last name?"

"No," Luther chuckles. "Do you?"

"I don't think any of us do," I say while shaking my head. "We all took turns with her but we don't even know who she is."

"That was the way that sort of party could be in college," Brenton replies. "It was nasty and straight to the point. I couldn't hold my beer too well back then and it got me into some trouble."

"Me too," Aiden admits. "I can't tell you how many times I went to bed with a supermodel and then woke up with an ugly woman." We all laugh.

"That's all you could ever get," Devin jokes. "All ugly women." We laugh as Aiden shakes his head. I do recall that he was quick to have sex with just about any woman willing to have sex with him. I'm not so certain that any of us were very choosy on who we fucked, though. A lot of my college years are a haze to me. But not April. She was hot.

"We almost have the whole crew ready to go," Luther tells us. "After Sarah talks to Mindy, we might be able to go ahead and make plans. I think it should happen in a large hotel room."

"Are hotel rooms big enough?" Aiden asks. "I was thinking maybe we could go to Brenton's house."

"My house?" He shakes his head. "You guys forget that I have a couple of children. I don't think that would be such a great idea."

"Get a babysitter to take them for the night," Devin replies. "Do we have to think of everything for ya?" Again, we all laugh. I feel so very at home with my old college buddies. I wonder what it will be like to have sex with their wives while they enjoy Mindy? There's still a chance that I will never know that feeling. After all, nothing is written in stone. Sarah might convince her, but then again she might not. I have to be willing to accept either outcome.

"I'll think about having it at my house. We would have to be careful not to disturb the neighborhood if we do. The neighbors are in our church."

I smile. "That would be interesting, huh? I'll bet they would peep if given the chance."

"Maybe so," Brenton answers with a grin. "But I would never be able to look them in the eyes again after that." We laugh again. Though I feel happy on the outside about the plans being made, I am more interested in seeing how things turn out with Mindy after Sarah speaks to her. Only time will tell.

Chapter Eight: Courtesy Call

The doorbell rings and I go to the door to greet Sarah. She called Mindy earlier to tell her she was coming over and wanted to speak with both of us.

"Hey, Sarah," I say as I feel my face turn a little pink. At five-seven and around one hundred thirty-five pounds, the beautiful brunette is attractive and athletic. Her warm hazel eyes look me over as she passes by me and into the living room before she speaks to me.

"Hello, Jordan. It's been a while."

I nod my head. "Yes, it has. I'm glad you got the chance to come over."

"Me too." She smiles and blushes a little as well as she turns to see Mindy walking into the living room. "There's the lady I've come to see." They embrace as I watch near the door.

"I was surprised to get your call," Mindy tells her. "We've not been in touch a lot lately."

"No, and I believe that's my fault," Sarah replies. "Brenton and I have just been so busy lately that we haven't had the opportunity to see our friends. That's about to change."

Mindy nods her head. "Oh, how rude of me. Please have a seat." My wife motions toward the sofa in the living room. "Would you like something to drink?"

"No, thank you," Sarah replies as she sits down on the sofa. "I need to speak to both of you, though." Her eyes turn to me for a moment. I move toward a chair nearby and sit down as my wife sits beside our guest.

"I hope all's well with you and Brenton." Mindy appears to be concerned that the other woman has decided to pay us a visit. Perhaps she thinks that Brenton has had an affair behind Sarah's back and their marriage is now over? I know the true purpose of this visit and goosebumps are rising along my body as I try to get comfortable.

"We're better than ever," she tells my wife. "As a matter of fact, that's part of the reason that I'm here." Mindy appears to be confused as she gets comfortable beside Sarah. "Brenton and I have recently had an epiphany of sorts and I wanted to share it with you."

"An epiphany? What do you mean?" I sit back as the two women begin to talk.

"Well, what I mean is that we have discovered that we have been very wrong about some things. So, we're trying to change what we do together. Part of that process needs you and Jordan to be involved." My body shakes a little as I watch Sarah begin to tee up the conversation. As I study her and the way that she interacts with Mindy, I begin to understand the bonds that only women can have with other women.

"What's going on between you?" Mindy asks.

Sarah clears her throat. "Brenton and I are beginning to look at our sexuality and what it means for the two of us. While doing this, we have come to a conclusion. We plan to be a part of the swingers party that the boys started talking about a few weeks ago. We need this, and to be honest, I think that the two of you need it too."

Mindy's face turns pale as she looks away from her friend. It's as if she has suddenly been struck with a surprise blow from someone near and dear to her. I'm sure my wife is trying to figure out what needs to be said and how she needs to say it as she considers Sarah's statement. I sit back and simply watch the exchange with intense interest.

"You know about that?" Mindy asks calmly.

Sarah smiles. "Brenton was approached several times about it and then we talked about what it would mean for us. The fact is, my husband and I have been wanting to find some way to express ourselves to each other in more meaningful ways. Unfortunately, there are limitations in doing that as long as we continue to fixate only on each other. I think Brenton noticed that before I did, and so he was convinced before I was. Now, though, I am fully committed to doing something sexually with another man. Even if that other man is Jordan."

"Jordan?" Mindy's eyes turn to look at me. "What has he done?"

"Nothing," Sarah replies. "He's told us that he can't take part in the swingers party because he doesn't want to offend you, Mindy. Your hubby is very devoted to you." The other woman turns and looks at me. "There was a time, even after I was married, that I wanted to have sex with Jordan. I didn't think I would admit that today, but here I am. Please forgive me." She turns her attention back to my wife.

"Um…" Mindy seems puzzled as to what she has heard so far. We have known Brenton and Sarah to be staunchly moral people. It was sort of the whole anchor for some parts of our existence. We could always use them as an example of someone we were not quite as prude as. At least, that's what Mindy would do. Now it seems that Sarah has admitted to wanting to screw me even while we were both married.

"Nothing has happened," I tell Mindy as I worry that she might get the wrong impression. "She's just here to talk."

Sarah gets up from her seat and looks down at my wife. "What would happen if Jordan had a sexual encounter with me, Mindy? How would that make you feel?"

Mindy looks at me and then up at her friend. "I don't know. Jordan wouldn't do that, though. He promised."

"I know." Sarah turns and walks over to where I am sitting. She goes to her knees and reaches for my pants. Her fingers begin to nimbly unbutton and then unzip the front of my blue jeans. I almost reach for her hands to push them away, but then she looks into my eyes and shakes her head. Brenton's wife aims to prove a point.

She reaches into my pants and finds my hardening shaft, pulling it out with her hand and then stroking it slowly. *"Fuck,"* I say as I look at her hand on my cock. It's been several years, since before I was married, that I've had another woman's hand on that part of my body.

"What are you doing?" Mindy seems alarmed as she sits forward on the sofa. "This isn't like you, Sarah."

"I know," she replies. "But Brenton and I have come to realize that we need more than just our wedding vows, Mindy. We need to know that we can have a great time with each other no matter the setting. We need to know that we can depend on each other even though we might want to pleasure someone else." She pulls up hard on my johnson, causing my body to buck a little as I pre-come. As Sarah slowly moves her hand over my natural lubricant, she smiles at me. It seems almost inconceivable that this could be happening right now.

"Your hands are so soft," I moan as Sarah places her other hand into my pants and pulls out my ball sack. She massages it as her other hand continues to move up and down my pole.

"Mindy, you have to let go. He's not your father and he loves you. It doesn't matter that I'm doing this for him right now. The fact that I'm going to make him come inside my hands has nothing to do with your vows. I'm going to make him come because I want to see Jordan come." She turns and looks at me again. "And he wants to come for me. It won't affect your marriage at all." Sarah moves her hand a little faster along my shaft and my toes begin to point. If she keeps this up, she will definitely cause me to to ejaculate.

"He's my husband," Mindy tells her. My wife then looks at me. "Stop that, Jordan. Don't come for her."

"I can't help it," I reply as I grit my teeth. "She's good at this. Her hands..." I stop talking as Sarah takes her hand over the tip of my dick. It's all I can do to keep myself from squirting right now. The young, athletic woman has a true talent for the way she is handling my penis.

"Dammit, Sarah. He's mine."

"And he'll be yours when he's finished," she replies. Mindy pulls up hard on my cock. "You're close, huh?" She smiles at me. "Do you want to come for me, Jordan? Do you want me to catch it for you?"

"I want to come," I say while closing my eyes.

"Come for me."

"Fuck..." Mindy says nothing more as I sit back and feel my balls pushing my white man gravy toward my erect rod. It doesn't take much longer for me to finally lose my wad as the two women look on. *"GAHHHH!!! AHHHHH!!!"* My body shakes violently as the first and second squirts from the tip of my cock fall onto Sarah's arm and shoulder. *"Oh, fuck...FUCK!!!"* My hands grip the edges of the chair as I empty my balls into her soft, beautiful hands. Sarah smiles as she watches my cock heave all of my balls' content onto her. It takes just seconds for her to milk every last drop from me.

Sarah pulls her hand away from my cock and reaches for some Kleenexes on the table nearby. After wiping her hands, she asks my wife, "What did you not like about what I did to Jordan?"

Mindy shakes her head. She still appears to be in disbelief over the whole episode. "You can't do that to a married man. We're friends, Sarah."

"Yes, and this didn't change that at all," Brenton's wife replies with a gentle smile. "Jordan came for me because of a physically sexual need that he has. It had nothing to do with whether he loves me or not. He doesn't. He just needed to be touched in a different way, and I did that for him."

"I can't believe you did that," she tells our guest. "What would Brenton say if he were here?"

"It was my husband's idea," Sarah informs her. "It's the only way either of us could come up with to get you to understand that sex and a deeper connection to your husband are two different things. Sure, they can happen together, but they often don't. I jerked off your husband, Mindy. What did you *like* about that?"

At first, I don't think that my wife would answer such a question. Then, she nods her head and says, "He really liked it, didn't he?"

"I think so," Sarah laughs as she looks at the mess on her shoulder and arm. "Does that turn you on?"

Mindy swallows hard as she looks at me. "A little. I guess." Something is changing inside my wife. I can tell that for the first time she's considering what it would be like for this to happen for us both at the same time. She hasn't thought about the swingers party in this way before, but now it has become more real for her. Will this bring her around to accepting the idea of a swingers party?

"You liked it too, Jordan? Did you like coming for both of us?"

"Yeah," I say as I nod my head. "I liked it a lot."

"And are you in love with me and want to leave Mindy?"

"No, of course not."

Sarah looks at my wife. "We can have sex without the feelings of love or commitment, Mindy. I know what happened with your father was traumatic, but it doesn't have to be your story with your husband. You are two different people and you both deserve to be treated as such." Sarah finishes cleaning herself up and then walks toward the door. "I hope to see you both at the party." She smiles and then lets herself out of our house as I pull my cock back into my pants.

There is silence in our living room at first as we each think quietly on what has happened. I am the first to say something. "We don't have to do it, Mindy. I would like to, but we don't have to. Whatever you want is what will happen."

She nods her head. "Thanks for that. But you came with her." My wife looks at me. "I don't think I ever believed you could do that."

"Yeah, that was a little different, huh?" I worry that what Sarah did to me might backfire. However, Mindy begins to smile.

"If I get there and just want to watch, is that okay?"

I sit up in my chair. "Of course."

Mindy nods her head. "I'm not sure that I can have sex with someone else, but I think I would like to see you have a little fun, Jordan. Would that be okay?"

"Yeah, that's fine." My heart races as I get excited about the thought of having sex with the other wives.

"Okay, then. Let's do it." Mindy's eyes look me over before she gets up and leaves the living room. My mind swims with thoughts about what has happened and how it has changed my wife's mind.

"Damn," I say to myself as I smile.

Chapter Nine: A Good Time for All

"A party boat?" Mindy's eyes grow large as we walk across the deck of the rental boat. "Who's paying for this?"

"We all are," I reply with a grin. "But it was Devin's idea after talking to Brenton. Apparently he knows someone who owns the company that rents these out. Pretty cool, eh?"

My wife giggles. "This seems so naughty, Jordan. It's all deck. There's no privacy except for the small cabin area." Mindy shakes her head. "Will the boat be out on the lake during the party?"

I nod my head. "Yeah, they're about to leave the dock. At least, we will once everyone is onboard."

"There you are!" Devin walks over to us and smiles. His wife Katie is right beside him and her cheeks blush as her blue eyes meet mine for a moment. My manhood springs to attention inside my shorts as I think about caressing her soft, naked body.

"We made it," I reply as I shake his hand. Katie and Mindy exchange a brief hug and I wonder if the two wives are thinking about what it would be like to have sex with each other's husbands. It's my guess that they probably are.

"Luther and Aiden are both here along with their wives." Devin motions toward the cabin where the two men are standing. Their wives are not on deck but must be inside the air conditioned cabin for the moment. The men wave at us and we wave back to them as Mindy squeezes my hand. She has agreed to come along for the swingers party, but she has told me that she will likely only watch. I wish she would change her mind about that, but I can't complain. Just a week ago she was still refusing to take part in the swingers party at all. At least this way she will be here and I will have the opportunity to enjoy some of the other wives.

Music starts to play on the speakers along the boat deck as the boat begins to move. "Wait, where's Brenton and Sarah?" Mindy asks as she looks around. "They are supposed to be here."

"We're here." We turn to see Sarah walking up to us. She gives Mindy and Katie each a quick embrace before turning to me and smiling. "Are you ready for this, Jordan?" The memory of how she squeezed my cock and caused me to come a few days ago is still fresh on my mind.

"I think so. Mindy seems a little apprehensive, but I'm ready."

"I'll watch," my wife says as she allows a half-smile. "That's all I need to do is watch."

"And then maybe you'll join in?" Katie asks. "We want everyone to take part, Mindy. even you."

She shakes her head. "I've got my reasons." Mindy then looks at me. "And I trust this guy. I guess it took Sarah showing me that I could trust him for us to be here at all."

"And let's get this show on the road," we suddenly hear Brenton say over the microphone. I'm surprised to see him take any sort of lead role in this party as it wasn't so long ago that he and his wife were opposed to taking part at all. However, I believe that Brenton and Sarah have agreed to pay for almost half the cost of the party boat on their own. They were probably happy to do it in order to keep it from happening at their house.

"Let's dance!" Lydia, Luther's wife, smiles as she carries a glass of wine across the boat's deck. We are soon served by a man in a white jacket as he walks out onto the deck behind her. The white wine is crisp and refreshing as I have a sip of it along with Mindy.

"Do you want to dance?" I ask my wife.

"Sure. I can do that." We put our wine glasses down on a table nearby and move toward the part of the deck where the others are dancing. I take Mindy's hand and twirl her around as the music plays loudly. It's been a long time since we have had this much fun together.

"Come on, people, is this a party or a funeral?" Katie, Devin's so-called prim and proper wife, is having more fun than I have seen her have before. There's just something about coming together for the purpose of having sex with other people. It's liberating. We all seem to get that sense. Except for Mindy.

"This is a little too weird," she tells me. "I haven't seen some of these women act like this before, Jordan. Are they on something?"

"They're not on drugs," I chuckle. "They have just decided that we aren't going to be so stiff and worried about what others might think. We're away from dry land, after all. No one is out here with us besides our friends and the ship's crew."

"The crew." Mindy frowns. "They're going to see everything that's going on, aren't they?"

"They have strict instructions to stay inside once things get going," Brenton says as he swings his wife around nearby. "Don't worry about them. It's just the ten of us." He smiles and pulls his wife tight to him before he begins to kiss her passionately. Then the tall man says, "Let's swap dance partners."

"What?" Mindy shakes her head.

"Sure. Why not." I don't give my wife the opportunity to refuse as I pass her off to Brenton and then take his wife into my arms.

"Hello again," Sarah says to me with a smile. "I hope you enjoyed our time together the last time we touched." She runs a hand along the side of my face and neck, causing goosebumps to form along my skin. To say that I'm sexually attracted to her would be an understatement. My balls literally ache to fill her with my seed."

"Hey, you changed dancer partners?" Katie raises an eyebrow as she moves away from Devin. "My turn." She gently nudges Sarah out of the way. I'm worried at first that Sarah might be offended, but she laughs it off and begins to dance with Devin.

"So, um, how have you been?" I ask Katie as she pulls close to me. The perfume on her body begins to turn me on as I look into her light blue eyes.

"Horny. And you?" She smiles wickedly as her hand slips into my shorts. Devin's wife finds my erect cock quickly and twists it inside her grip. "You're big, Jordan. Bigger than I thought you'd be."

"Wow." I pant hard as her hand slips past my rod and goes to my balls. Katie gently cradles my scrotum and massages it, a smile on her face.

"I have wanted you for a while," she tells me. Katie kisses me hard as I recall that Devin mentioned she was a bit of a nympho. My body quickly reacts as I pre-come onto her wrist and I hump a couple of times in her direction.

"Katie," I moan as she pulls my cock out and looks at it.

"Would you like to fuck me, Jordan?" She kisses the side of my neck as she whispers to me. "I'm waxed and ready. You can eat me out or fuck me. Whatever you want, baby. My asshole is yours too."

"Oh, shit." I continue to breathe hard as she goes to her knees and tugs on my cock. Devin's wife kisses the tip of my johnson before opening her mouth and taking me in. I nearly explode into her mouth as she sucks hard on me.

I turn and look over to see Devin with Sarah. The two of them are kissing deeply as they run their hands over each other's bodies. It's apparent that the two of them are very into each other, which makes me even harder as Katie continues to siphon my manly hose. On the other side of me are Mindy and Brenton. To my surprise, she's touching the bulge in his shorts. It's much more than I could have expected of my wife during this party. If she goes much further, it would be a complete surprise to me, though.

Katie stands up and pulls her shirt over her head. She is wearing a small black bra underneath that covers her C-cup breasts. As she smiles at me, Devin's wife quickly removes the bra as well so that I can see her taut pink nipples. She pulls my hand up and places it on one of them. "Natural, Jordan. And for now, all yours." I reach down and pull at her miniskirt, easily dropping it to the deck along with her thong panties. Her bald muff is beautiful as I sink a finger into it and feel its warm wetness. It's been so long since I felt any other woman's pussy besides Mindy's.

"I want you," I say quietly to Katie as I let her pull my tee shirt over my head. There are others on the boat already sharing each other's wives now as our naked bodies rake against each other.

"Brenton." I look over and see a strained look on my wife's face as the tall man's hand is deep inside her shorts. He's found her lady bit and he intends to pleasure her. Our eyes meet for one moment, and I can see that Mindy is now likely to give in fully to the swinging scene on the boat. She can't go back to refusing to take part in sex now. Not with Brenton making her feel so good.

"Take me, Jordan." I turn my attention back to Katie. She has leaned over one of the tables on the boat's deck, her pussy lips blooming out toward me as if inviting me to sink my pecker between them. That's just what I do as I run my finger along her bleached and puckered asshole.

"Shit, you're tight," I moan as I push my cock into her small pussy. Katie's body bucks as she feels the girth of my pole. I look up to see that Devin's cock is inside Sarah's sweet muff as well. She's lying back on a deck lounger as my friend slowly thrusts in and out of her. He looks over at me and smiles, nodding his approval of the way that I'm screwing his attractive wife. This makes me so horny that I have to slow my own thrusts so that I don't come too soon.

"Fuck me hard," Katie whimpers as she reaches between her legs and fondles her clit. "Fuck me really hard, Jordan. I can take it. Make me come really hard with you. Fuck me hard." She reaches back and spreads her ass cheeks, revealing her asshole and pussy more than before. She is obviously the nympho that her husband claimed she was earlier.

"Oh, *fuck!*" I look toward Mindy and see her naked with her legs around Brenton's waist. He's holding her up as his giant cock goes in and out of her pussy. *"Fuck...oh, fuck!"* My wife's face scrunches as she tries to take all of the other man's shaft into her pussy. He's fucking her so hard that his balls are slapping against her asshole. It's the sort of fantasy that I've dreamt of over the years. To see Mindy fucked by another man with such gusto is a real treat for me.

"Uh...I'm going to come!" I look over to see Aiden being serviced by Lydia, Luther's wife. It appears that they have swapped their wives and Aiden is getting his cock siphoned. He grits his teeth as he puts his hand on her head. "Fuck...*AHHHH!!!*" He begins to come inside her mouth. As he does, he pulls hard on her head, forcing his large cock to the back of her throat. Lydia struggles and pushes back against him, but he's too involved in his own orgasm to care. "*Ohhhh...uhhhh...fuck...AHHHH!!!*"

"*ACK!!!*" Lydia gags as some of Aiden's man gravy oozes from her mouth and drips to the ship's deck. "*UHT...*"

"Jordan." Katie turns to look at me. "Fuck me harder. *Much* harder." I put my hands on her soft, tanned hips and pull the young woman toward me. I can suddenly feel her cervix hit the end of my cock hard. "*OWWWW!!! Fuck, YES!!! HARDER!!!*" My balls ache as I do as she asks, ramming my hardness into her firm cervical ring. This is the sort of thing that Mindy never likes, so getting to hammer another woman's cervix is a treat for me. It feels so good against my swollen head as I get as deep as I can into Katie's pussy.

"You're so fucking hot." Brenton has his cock inside Mindy's asshole now, her legs pushed far back as she rests on the top of a table. My wife winches as he thrusts hard and fast inside her anus.

"Brenton...*fuck.*" Mindy looks at me, her eyes affixed on my cock. She watches for a moment as I fuck her friend. She seems to like it as I enjoy the feeling of Katie's vagina tightly wrapped around my johnson. "*Uhhhh...AHHHH!!!*" Mindy comes hard with Brenton as his jism begins to spill from her hole. "*Motherfucker!*" I smile as I have rarely heard her say such a thing, even during sex. Whatever the big guy is doing to her is working. He doesn't say much as he fills her void with his DNA soup. It's what I have wanted to see and I'm glad that Mindy is getting spunked into by my old friend.

"Holy...*SHIT!!!*" Devon suddenly comes as he fucks Sarah hard on the deck lounge nearby. They have switched positions and she's on top now. She seems like the controlling sort of woman, anyway. "*FUCK!!!*

Oh, shit...FUCK!!!" His toes point hard as Katie looks over at them. Her husband is creaming another woman's hole with his sauce. She smiles a little as she grinds her ass into me.

"Finger my ass," Katie groans. "Help me finish off, Jordan." I do as she asks, licking my finger first and then inserting it into her tight sphincter. Her body bucks a little as she continues to play with her clit and I fuck her pussy.

"UHHHH!!!" Luther comes in Aiden's wife, Rebecca, as he fucks her from behind. *"Yeah...YEAH!!!"* He tugs at the beautiful woman as he fills her tight muff. She comes with him as well, her body quaking with an orgasm. Everyone seems to be coming except for me.

"Jordan, I'm coming. Come with me. Come...*OOOOHHHHH...*" Katie squeaks as I fuck her hard, her pussy undulating around my cock as I thrust faster and harder than before. *"JORDAN!!! JORDAN!!!"* She calls my name out over and over again as I screw her from behind. My balls tighten and I begin to feel my own orgasm coming on as I pull hard on her hips.

"Uhhh...uhhhhh..." My face turns red as I put a hand on Katie's back and hold her down. *"Fuck...fuck...fuck...fuck..."* Each thrust goes along with every spurt from my pecker into Devin's wife. I come hard inside her and as I look down I can see some of my spunk creeping out of her sweet pussy. It's been a long time since I've ejaculated this much into any woman, including my own wife. I have fantasized about this for so long.

"Holy fuck." Devin gets up and walks over just as I finish up with his wife. I pull out of Katie and step back, a string of my own jism dripping from the tip of my dick to the boat deck below. "Are you okay, baby?"

Katie smiles and looks at me as she gets up off the table. "It was good, sweetie. Really good." She kisses her husband as I have a seat at another table. There is still some sex going on, but many of us have finished the first round. I get the feeling that this won't be the only time, though. We have the boat rented for six hours, so there's going to be plenty of time for second and third pops.

"She's a wild woman," Brenton says as he sits down nearby. His cock is flaccid now and Mindy is lying back on the table, her hands on her chest. She normally does rest a few minutes after sex with me, so I understand what she's doing. "You're a lucky man."

"And you are too," I chuckle. "Your wife gives really great head."

He smiles. "She said that she might do that when I suggested it to her. I thought you two would end up fucking just now, but I guess Devin's wife had other plans."

I nod my head. "She's apparently wanted me for a while." My cock flexes a little as the beautiful woman looks my way.

"Good thing that the party is just now beginning, huh?" Brenton smiles and gets up from his seat. He goes to another wife and begins to dance with her.

"And so it continues," I say with a smile on my face.

Chapter Ten: Greatly Anticipated

Mindy is quiet as we sit in our bedroom early the next morning. The night was long and full of sex and drinking, so her quiet attitude doesn't really surprise me. However, she soon begins to speak.

"I'm sorry if I caused you a lot of trouble about the whole party thing, Jordan."

I reach over and put my hand on hers. "You didn't cause me any trouble, Mindy. You weren't really wanting to do it at first. We all understood that. Hell, it took Brenton and Sarah a while to want to be a part of it, too."

My wife's face turns a little pink. "Brenton."

"You really had some fun with him, didn't you?"

Mindy blushes even more. "And with Devin. I can't believe that he wanted me to suck his dick."

"Ah, he had *Sarah* still on it." I laugh as I shake my head. "You did it anyway, right?"

"Shut up." Mindy smacks my hand with hers but then lays it back down on mine. "You're a crazy guy, Jordan."

"And apparently you're just as crazy as me, my love. You had a great time just like I did. We got to have sex with other people."

She nods her head. "It was much better than I thought it could possibly be. I expected to sit back and watch everyone else on the boat. I also thought it would be more oral stuff than it turned out to be. Some of you had some rough sex, Jordan." After fucking Katie, I decided Lydia would be my next conquest. She's small and easy to hold up, so we had sex while I held her on my cock. It was easy to move around on the deck with each other as I thrust in and out of her. I came while close to Mindy and Devin as they were having sex with each other.

"I want to consider doing it again," I inform my wife. "At least, in a month or so, after we have had time to recover from last night's party."

"With the others?"

"With a different group," I reply. "I want us to join a swingers group online and go to some of their parties. Just for a little variety."

Mindy's eyes grow wider. "Are you serious? You want to have sex with people we don't know?"

"People we don't know *yet*," I reply. "We would get to know them through the online forums. Honey, most of our friends won't do this again. Brenton and Sarah, for example, said at the end of the party that they have no interest in having a swingers party again any time soon. We need to find others who are willing to do it."

"I don't know."

"Just think about it, alright? I don't need an answer from you right now." I smile at Mindy as I put my arm around her. "Besides, I want to see you with another man again. That really turned me on, honey."

"It turned me on a little too." She smiles and adds, "I'll think about it, okay? Maybe in a few days I can give you an answer."

"That's all I ask." I hug my wife tightly as I think about last night on the boat. The swingers party was a wild success, but one that included just our closest friends. I want to go to one at which I can fuck someone I really don't know very well yet. That idea turns me on the most as I think about it. There are plenty of swingers groups out there looking for new members to add to their rolls. Hopefully my wife and I will be new members of one of those groups very soon. I'll have to wait for Mindy's answer before I know for certain.

THE END

Don't miss out!

Visit the website below and you can sign up to receive emails whenever Karly Violet publishes a new book. There's no charge and no obligation.

https://books2read.com/r/B-A-GIXE-IDTQB

About the Author

Sign up to my mailing list to receive the two free epilogues for 'A Hotwife Adventure' and 'Hotwife Training' and to stay up to date on all of my latest releases! http://eepurl.com/c3ICWf Sign up to my Patreon account and receive exclusive Hotwife stories every month and sexy scenes every week! https://www.patreon.com/karlyviolet

Read more at https://www.patreon.com/karlyviolet.

About the Publisher